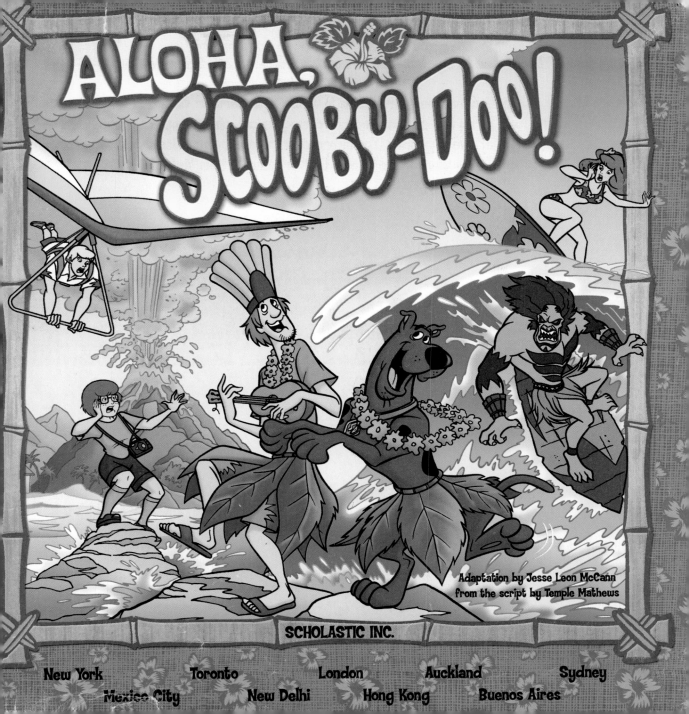

ALOHA, SCOOBY-DOO!

Adaptation by Jesse Leon McCann
from the script by Temple Mathews

SCHOLASTIC INC.

New York   Toronto   London   Auckland   Sydney
Mexico City   New Delhi   Hong Kong   Buenos Aires

ISBN 0-439-70429-4

Copyright © 2004 by Hanna-Barbera.

"Aloha, Scooby-Doo!" © 2004 Warner Home Video.

SCOOBY-DOO and all related characters and elements are trademarks of and © Hanna-Barbera.

(s04)

Published by Scholastic Inc. All rights reserved.

SCHOLASTIC and associated logos are trademarks and/or registered trademarks of Scholastic Inc.

Cover and interior illustration
by Duendes del Sur

Designed by Louise Bova & Amy Heinrich

12 11 10 9 8 7 6 5 4 3   5 6 7 8 9/0

Printed in the U.S.A.
First printing, December 2004

Scooby-Doo and his friends were on vacation in Hawaii. The girls took pictures in the jungle while the boys learned to hang glide.

"Like, how do you land these things?" Shaggy hollered.

"I don't know," Fred said.

"Ruh-roh!" Scooby cried. Luckily, he and Shaggy landed without getting too many bumps.

3

The gang moved on to a town that was holding a big surfing contest. But something strange was happening there. Almost everyone was leaving! Nearby, a man named Jared was busy selling good-luck charms.

"Beware of Hawaii's most terrifying spirit!" Jared warned. "Get your Wikki Tikki charms now!"

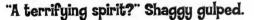

"A terrifying spirit?" Shaggy gulped.

"Angry Wikki Tikki spirits live in the volcano," Jared explained. "Legend says they must be soothed with a human sacrifice!"

Two local surfers, Manu and Little Jim, had more bad news. Earlier, Wikki Tikki spirits had kidnapped Manu's girlfriend, Snookie!

"Well gang, it looks like we've got another mystery on our hands," Fred declared.

The mayor and a local businessman named Ruben didn't believe in the Wikki Tikki curse. They thought Snookie would show up sooner or later. To calm everyone's nerves, they threw a big luau party that night. There was dancing, games, and lots of food. Shaggy and Scooby really loved that!

But their good time was ruined when Wikki Tikki spirits attacked! "Snarf! Growl! Wikki Tikki!" the little creatures snarled.
"What in the world are those things?" Fred exclaimed.
"I don't know, and I don't want to find out!" cried Shaggy.

The gang managed to escape the Wikki Tikki, but the luau was ruined.

The next day, Scooby and Shaggy wanted to go out surfing. They figured it would be safe, but they were wrong. A huge Wikki Tikki monster riding a surfboard attacked them! "Rrowl! Snarl!"

Luckily, Shaggy and Scooby were able to catch a big wave and escape just in the nick of time.

Manu agreed to take the gang into the jungle, where a mysterious medicine woman named Auntie Mahina lived. Manu said that Auntie might be able to help them solve the Wikki Tikki mystery and rescue Snookie.

But in the thickest part of the jungle, Manu heard a Wikki Tikki spirit growling! He ran ahead to fight it, and he never came back. It seemed the Wikki Tikki had captured him, too!

The gang had to go on without Manu. Soon they came to a rickety bridge. One at a time, they crossed over. Unfortunately, when it was Daphne's turn, she fell right through!

Thinking quickly, Daphne grabbed a rope that hung from the bridge's edge. Then she swung to safety.

On the other side of the bridge, the gang finally found Auntie Mahina's shack. When she learned that Manu and Snookie were kidnapped by the Wikki Tikki, Auntie began a spooky ritual.

"The Wikki Tikki is angry!" Auntie cried. "You must save Manu and Snookie from its lair inside the mountain!"

Auntie Mahina gave Fred an amulet to protect the gang from Wikki Tikki spirits and sent them on their way. Following her directions, they found themselves deep within the mountain volcano. But they weren't alone!

"Bats," Velma whispered. "Be very quiet, or we'll spook them."

Just then, Scooby felt a tickle inside his nose. He needed to sneeze!

Ah-ah-ah-choo!

Thousands of startled bats swarmed all around the gang! They fled through twisting, turning, underground chambers until they escaped the bats.

"Yuck!" Shaggy said. "Any more of that, and I'd have gone batty!"

The path turned to stone steps. Suddenly, Wikki Tikki spirits appeared all around, snarling and throwing spears!

"These creepy Tikkis are everywhere, man!" Shaggy cried. "We're doomed!"

Luckily, Scooby found a hidden passage. The gang hid there as the creatures passed right by them.

The gang continued on, and the sights became more wondrous.
"Look at these carvings!" Velma exclaimed. "They're beautiful!"
Up ahead, they made an amazing discovery. Manu's girlfriend,
Snookie, was standing near the Wikki Tikki sacrificial altar!
But Snookie screamed and ran away when she saw them.
"The poor thing is terrified," Daphne said. "We've got to save her!"

But saving Snookie would have to wait. The huge
Wikki Tikki monster appeared, leaping toward the gang.
Fred pulled out Auntie Mahina's good-luck charm and
held it out at the creature. "Stay back!" he shouted.
The Wikki Tikki came closer, growling and howling.
The amulet wasn't working!

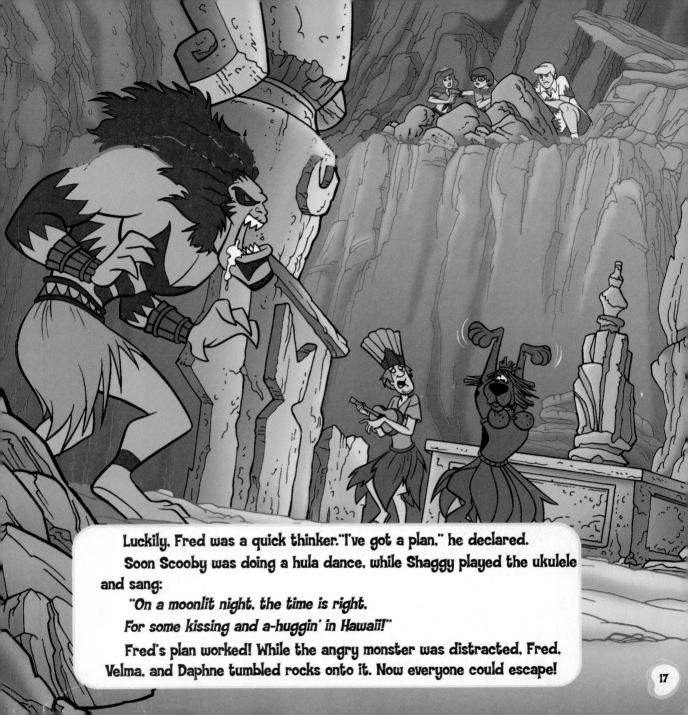

Luckily, Fred was a quick thinker. "I've got a plan," he declared.

Soon Scooby was doing a hula dance, while Shaggy played the ukulele and sang:

"On a moonlit night, the time is right,
For some kissing and a-huggin' in Hawaii!"

Fred's plan worked! While the angry monster was distracted, Fred, Velma, and Daphne tumbled rocks onto it. Now everyone could escape!

The huge Wikki Tikki broke free of the rocks, grabbed Snookie, and disappeared behind a heavy stone door. The gang tried to follow them. Unfortunately, they came across a very big problem!

"A s-snake pit!" Shaggy cried. "Oh man, I hate snakes!"

"By the looks of it, they're not exactly fond of you, either!" Daphne replied.

Since snakes can be charmed by music, Shaggy played his ukulele and sang again. The angry snakes calmed down, and began to sway from side to side. The gang sneaked past the slithery serpents to safety.

"Let's get out of here!" Fred began to run, and the others followed.

Fred and the girls saw that they were running toward the edge of a cliff that dropped away to a river. They were able to stop in time, but Shaggy and Scooby smacked into them from behind. They all tumbled into the river below. *Splash!*

The rushing river swiftly carried them away, around boulders and down waterfalls. Finally, it dumped them ashore near an underground tunnel.

"We'll never find Snookie and Manu now," Velma said.

Scooby and his pals saw light inside the tunnel, so they walked toward it. They never would have guessed what was inside – little Wikki Tikkis!

"Shhh! You'll wake them up," Shaggy warned.

"They're not asleep," Velma said. "They're not even real. They're robots!"

"Hey! Look at this!" Fred exclaimed. "When hot water is poured into this pool, it makes steam! This volcano isn't smoking at all!"

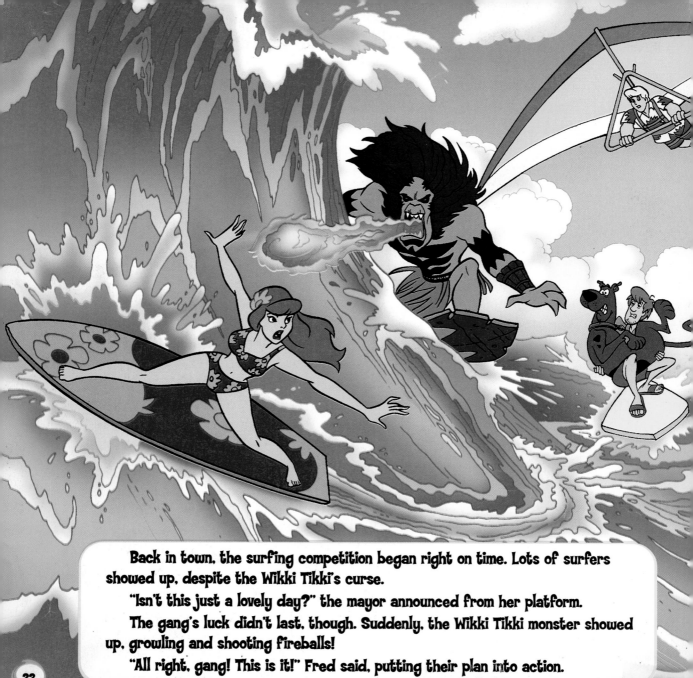

Back in town, the surfing competition began right on time. Lots of surfers showed up, despite the Wikki Tikki's curse.

"Isn't this just a lovely day?" the mayor announced from her platform.

The gang's luck didn't last, though. Suddenly, the Wikki Tikki monster showed up, growling and shooting fireballs!

"All right, gang! This is it!" Fred said, putting their plan into action.

Scooby-Doo, Shaggy, and Daphne acted as bait, surfing out on the water. Fred attacked from above on his hang glider. The creature became so distracted, it wiped out!

"Like, totally radical, Scoob!" Shaggy grinned and high-fived Scooby.

Velma pulled off the Wikki Tikki's mask to reveal Manu underneath! "Manu and Snookie were behind it all along, trying to scare off the locals and buy their homes for pennies!" Velma explained.

"Our plan would have worked, too, if it weren't for you meddling mainlanders," Manu grumbled, as the police took him and Snookie away.

That evening, the town threw another luau to celebrate the end of the Wikki Tikki curse. Everybody partied, danced, and ate delicious Hawaiian goodies. And nobody had a better time than Scooby-Doo!